E COW
Cowell, Cressida.
Don't do that, Kitty Kilroy

DATE DUE

For Maisie –
C.C.

Copyright © 1999 by Cressida Cowell
First American edition 2000 published by Orchard Books
First published in Great Britain in 1999 by Hodder Children's Books

Orchard Books, A Grolier Company
95 Madison Avenue, New York, NY 10016

Printed in Hong Kong
The text of this book is set in 26 point New Baskerville.
The illustrations are pen and ink and watercolor.

1 3 5 7 9 10 8 6 4 2

Library of Congress Cataloging-in-Publication Data
Cowell, Cressida.
Don't do that, Kitty Kilroy!/ by Cressida Cowell.—lst American ed.   p.   cm.
Summary: Kitty Kilroy wishes her mother would go away so that she would stop telling
Kitty what not to do.
ISBN 0-531-30209-1 (trade only : alk. paper)
[1. Behavior—Fiction. 2. Mother and child—Fiction.] I. Title.
PZ7.C83535Do 1999 [E]—dc21 99-25546

Don't do that, Kitty Kilroy!

Cressida Cowell

Orchard Books • New York

All day long Kitty's mom says,

Don't do that, Kitty Kilroy!

When Kitty puts her feet on the couch,

Don't do that, Kitty Kilroy!

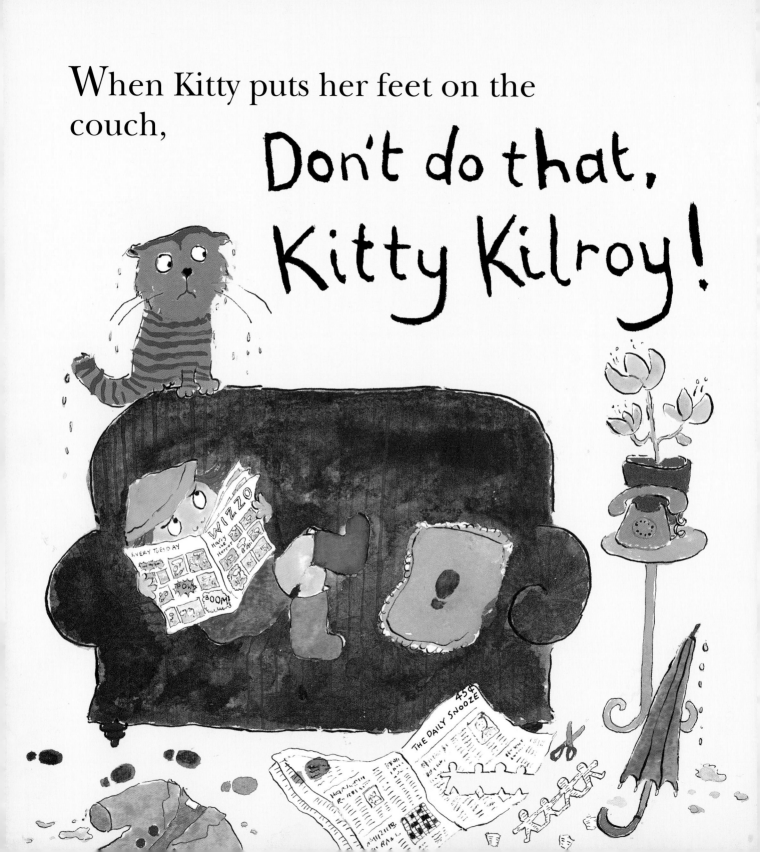

When Kitty eats food that is bad for her teeth,

Don't do that, Kitty Kilroy!

When Kitty makes a big mess in the living room,

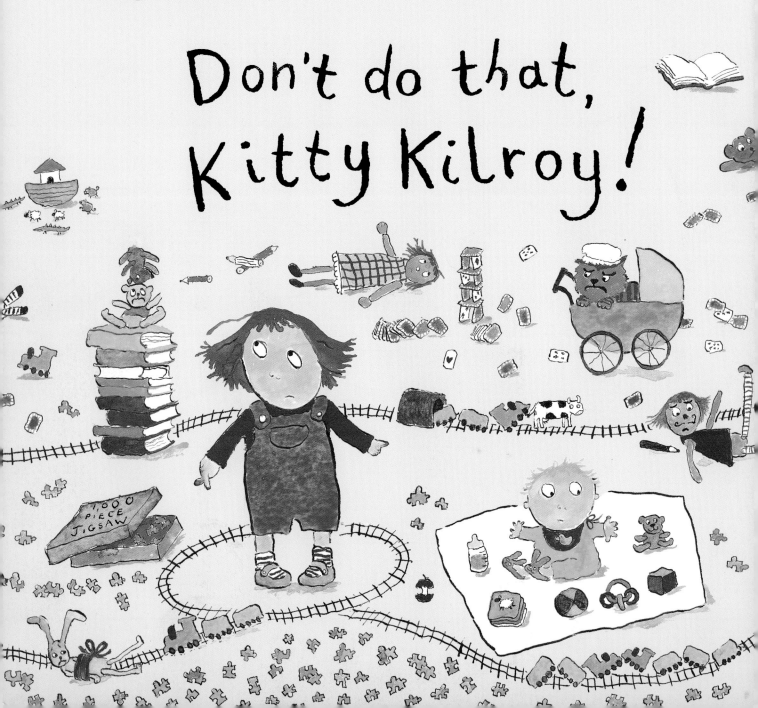

Don't do that, Kitty Kilroy!

One day Kitty had had enough.

Why don't you go away and let me do what I want?

So Kitty's mother DID go away . . .

. . . and Kitty did what she wanted.

She wore pajamas all day long.

She ate nothing but cereal and
ice cream . . .

which gave her lots of energy.

She watched television for hours
and hours.

She called up all her friends . . .

. . . and invited them over to help her
mess up the living room . . .

and stay up way past their bedtimes.

After a while it was no fun anymore.

Suddenly they heard footsteps . . .

. . . and there was Kitty's mother.

Z..z..z..z..z...

What do you want to do now, Kitty Kilroy?

Kitty's mother sent Kitty's friends home
to their mothers.

Kitty's mom washed Kitty's face. And she gave Kitty some medicine to make her feel better.

Sleep tight, Kitty Kilroy.

She put Kitty to bed, which was just what Kitty wanted.

Until tomorrow of course. . . .